Animal Cake Day

Written by Hannah Fish
Illustrated by David Hurtado

Collins

Who and what is in this story?

Listen and say

Mum

Dad

Sammy

Sally

cake

Download the audio at www.collins.co.uk/839708

animals

🎧 It is Animal Cake Day at school.
Sally and Sammy are making cakes.

Sammy says, "I've got chocolate for my cake."

Me too!

Sally says, "I've got chocolate *and* bananas for my cake!"

Sammy says, "Oh! I've got chocolate, bananas *and* a pear!"

Sally says, "Well, I've got four eggs!"

Sammy says, "Well, I've got five ...
Oh no! My eggs!"

Sally says, "Don't worry, here you are."

Sammy says, "Thank you, Sally! What animal cake are you making?"

Sally says, "My animal is yellow and black!"

13

Sally says, "No, it isn't. It's small and it can fly!"

Sally says, "No, it isn't! It's a bee!"

Sammy says, "My animal is big and brown."

Is it a bear?

Sammy says, "No, it isn't. It's got a long tail."

Sally says, "Is it a monkey?
I love monkeys!"

Sammy says, "Yes, it is!
I love monkeys, too!"

21

Picture dictionary

Listen and repeat

banana

cake

chocolate

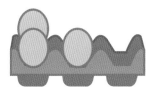

eggs

pear

1 Look and order the story

2 Listen and say

Collins

Published by Collins
An imprint of HarperCollins*Publishers*
Westerhill Road
Bishopbriggs
Glasgow
G64 2QT

HarperCollins*Publishers*
1st Floor, Watermarque Building
Ringsend Road
Dublin 4
Ireland

William Collins' dream of knowledge for all began with the publication of his first book in 1819.

A self-educated mill worker, he not only enriched millions of lives, but also founded a flourishing publishing house. Today, staying true to this spirit, Collins books are packed with inspiration, innovation and practical expertise. They place you at the centre of a world of possibility and give you exactly what you need to explore it.

© HarperCollins*Publishers* Limited 2020

10 9 8 7 6 5 4 3 2

ISBN 978-0-00-839708-1

Collins® and COBUILD® are registered trademarks of HarperCollins*Publishers* Limited

www.collins.co.uk/elt

British Library Cataloguing in Publication Data

A catalogue record for this publication is available from the British Library.

Author: Hannah Fish
Illustrator: David Hurtado (Beehive)
Series editor: Rebecca Adlard
Publishing manager: Lisa Todd
Product managers: Jennifer Hall and Caroline Green
In-house editor: Alma Puts Keren
Project manager: Emily Hooton
Editor: Tessie Papadopoulou-Dalton
Proofreaders: Natalie Murray and Michael Lamb
Cover designer: Kevin Robbins
Typesetter: 2Hoots Publishing Services Ltd
Audio produced by id audio, London
Reading guide author: Emma Wilkinson
Production controller: Rachel Weaver
Printed and bound by: GPS Group, Slovenia

Download the audio for this book and a reading guide for parents and teachers at www.collins.co.uk/839708